The HARLEM NUTCRACKER

BASED ON THE BALLET BY
DONALD BYRD

TEXT AND PHOTOGRAPHY BY
SUSAN KUKLIN

JUMP AT THE SUN
HYPERION BOOKS FOR CHILDREN • NEW YORK

Remembering our grandmothers,
Esther Rowe
—D.B.
Sarah Gussman
—S.K.

Text © 2001 by Donald Byrd and Susan Kuklin

Photographs © 2001 by Susan Kuklin

First Edition

1 3 5 7 9 10 8 6 4 2

Library of Congress Cataloging-in-Publication Data

Byrd, Donald.

The Harlem Nutcracker / Donald Byrd and Susan Kuklin; photographs by Susan Kuklin.

p.   cm.

Summary: A retelling of the classic story of Tchaikovsky's Nutcracker ballet, featuring an African American grandmother and her family and set in Harlem.

ISBN 0-7868-0633-8 (hc)

[1. Christmas—Fiction. 2. Grandmothers—Fiction. 3. Afro-Americans—Fiction. 4. Harlem (New York, New York)—Fiction.] I. Kuklin, Susan. II. Title.

PZ7.K9490147 Har 2001

   [Fic]—dc21

      00-46172

Visit www.jumpatthesun.com

The HARLEM NUTCRACKER

CHOREOGRAPHED AND DIRECTED BY DONALD BYRD

THE CAST

CLARA . . . . ELEANOR MCCOY

GUS, CLARA'S HUSBAND/THE NUTCRACKER . . . . GUS SOLOMONS, JR.

LAKEY, THEIR DAUGHTER . . . . LAKEY EVANS

JAMAL, THEIR SON-IN-LAW . . . . JAMAL STORY

LISA, THEIR DAUGHTER-IN-LAW . . . . LISA JOHNSON

THADDEUS, THEIR SON . . . . THADDEUS DAVIS

DOMINICAN NEIGHBORS

HUSBAND . . . . ROGER BELLAMY

WIFE . . . . ALEXANDRA DAMIANI

GRANDFATHER . . . . FREDDIE MOORE

HOMEYS

HUSBAND . . . . DEVIN PULLINS

WIFE . . . . KEMBA SHANNON

DEATH . . . . GREGORY KING

CHILDREN
THE ELLINGTON CHILDREN'S DANCERS

CHORUS
THE WOOTEN CHORAL ENSEMBLE

The first snow of winter fell softly past the windows of the spacious Sugar Hill mansion in Harlem. Inside, Clara was alone, lost in thought. It was Christmas Eve, a magical night for Clara and her family. Her daughter and son and their families would soon arrive to celebrate the holiday. Carolers and friends and neighbors would drop by for dancing and sweets and exchanging gifts.

Christmas Eve was special for another reason. On this day, many years ago, Clara's beloved Gus had asked for her hand in marriage.

She gazed at the portrait of her husband, draped in black above the fireplace. This was her first Christmas without him. She missed him. She missed the life they shared. Her Gus, her prince.

"Clara," came a whisper.

Suddenly, Gus appeared in a brilliant blue light, looking just as he had the Christmas before. Clara ran to his embrace.

"You don't think I'd leave my Clara alone on Christmas Eve?" Gus said, laughing.

They danced together and finished trimming the tree. With a grand gesture, Gus presented Clara with a large box.

Clara opened it. It was a nutcracker, the very one Gus had given her on Christmas Eve, many years before.

While she admired the nutcracker, Gus slipped a ring on her finger—just as he had long ago. "I am always with you, my darling," he told her.

But when the doorbell rang, Gus vanished as quickly as he'd appeared. Feeling lonely again, Clara answered the door.

"Mother!" It was her beautiful and very pregnant daughter, Lakey. Behind her, Lakey's husband, Jamal, and their two children were all smiles and frosty breaths.

"Grandma Clara!" they shouted. Clara gave each one a big hug, as only a grandmother can.

The doorbell rang again. "This must be Thaddeus and Lisa and the kids," Clara said. Lakey rolled her eyes. "Please, Lakey, be nice," Clara urged. "Can't we all get along, just this one night?"

"Mother, I try," Lakey replied. "But you know how Lisa is, she thinks she's better than everyone else. Everything's me! me! me!"

"Hush," said Clara, walking toward the door. "Your brother adores her. And she loves him. That is what's important."

Lisa dashed in, her family in tow. She quickly took over Clara's house, rearranging the sweets table, puffing the pillows, straightening her son's tie, tightening her daughter's pigtails, all the while chattering away nonstop. Only the ringing of the doorbell stopped her banter.

"I'll get it," Lisa called. Lakey gave her mother a long see-what-I-mean look.

Soon the parlor was filled with family and friends. Clara's Dominican neighbors arrived, with presents and hugs, wishing a *feliz Navidad.* Everyone liked the Dominicans because they were kind and they were fun. Lisa liked them because they were rich.

Ring, ring, ring. "More visitors!" sang Lisa, rushing to the door. This family was not rich. Lisa slammed the door in their faces.

"Let them in, Lisa!" Thaddeus demanded. "They are our friends. This is Christmas Eve, for goodness' sake." Grudgingly, she opened the door.

"Yo! Who do you think you are, girl?" Clara's neighbors were shouting mad.

"Please, everyone," Clara cried. "Peace!" Everyone quieted down. The last thing they wanted was to make Clara's Christmas Eve harder than it already was.

The carolers arrived in the nick of time:

SING OUT!
LET EV'RYONE HEAR
THE GOSPEL OF CHEER
THE TIDINGS OF JOY!

SING OUT
LIKE ANGELS ABOVE
A CAROL OF LOVE
TO THE CHILDREN OF HARLEM!

Sensing that their mother was feeling sad, Lakey and Thaddeus tried to distract her. "Mama, will you dance with us—just like you did when we were kids?"

Then the children took over the parlor with a foot-stomping, *shu-bah*-thumping hip-hop dance. The room filled with laughter and happiness.

While everyone was dancing, Lisa was sipping the punch. "I'm ready to dance!" she announced, whipping off her jacket.

Lisa twisted, staggered, then tripped. "I have it . . . I . . . I . . . I . . . I don't have it," she muttered and sputtered and swooned.

Clara was upset by her daughter-in-law's behavior, and Lakey was furious. The guests decided it was time to leave.

One by one, Clara's children and grandchildren headed upstairs to bed, leaving Clara alone once again.

The house on Sugar Hill was as quiet as the falling snow. With her husband gone and her daughter and daughter-in-law at odds, Clara worried that she could not hold the family together. Unable to sleep, she began tidying up. Suddenly, a sharp pain pierced her heart. She cried out, but no one could hear her.

Out of the shadows emerged a gruesome face. Death.

"No!" gasped Clara. Somehow, she thought, the nutcracker would protect her. Clara crawled to the sofa and clutched the nutcracker. The pain subsided. But just as she was about to go upstairs, Death entered the parlor.

"No, please. Not yet. My family needs me," she wailed. The more she resisted Death, the more terrifying it became.

"Help!" Clara cried.

The nutcracker sprang to life! He defended Clara fearlessly.

Death called for reinforcements, a battalion of ghouls. But they were no match for the nutcracker.

Then Death itself stepped in. The nutcracker was very brave, but he could not fight off the powerful, eternal force.

Clara hastened to the nutcracker's side. Taking his battered head in her arms, she tenderly removed his mask.

She was amazed to see the face of her husband, her beloved Gus, emerge from the broken nutcracker.

"Ooooweee," Gus groaned, rubbing his head, "do I have a headache!" Clara laughed and cried at the same time.

"My darling," he said, beaming, "I tried to save you—and you saved me." Gus took Clara into his arms and they danced into the Harlem night.

A crowd of revelers joined Gus and Clara in the celebration of Christmas and love. As they danced, Gus offered to take Clara anywhere she wanted to go. "Anywhere, anytime, anyplace."

"How about Club Sweets?" Clara suggested. Club Sweets, the marvelous nightclub in Clara's mother's time, had always had the hottest jazz and the coolest crowd.

"Your wish is my command," Gus replied.

But when they tried to enter the club, the doorman had other ideas. "I don't think so," said the doorman. "You are not the kind we want in this-here joint."

When Clara's husband pulled out a wad of bills, the doorman took it all. "*Now* you are the kind we want in this-here joint."

"Welcome! Welcome!" The patrons greeted Clara and Gus. "We don't know who you are, but you must be *somebody*, or you wouldn't be here. So elegant! So happy! So in love!"

At Club Sweets, everyone leaves their troubles behind. At Club Sweets, Clara is young and beautiful. At Club Sweets, Gus is handsome and alive. At Club Sweets, life is beautiful. At Club Sweets, it's . . .

"SHOW TIME!"

First, a magician performed the most miraculous feats of wizardry. When he called for a volunteer, Clara boldly stepped up.

He waved his magic wand. ABRACADABRA ABRACAZAM! PRESTO! Clara disappeared. The crowd oohed and aahed. CADABRA CADABRA CAZAM! PRESTO! She returned to the cheers of the crowd.

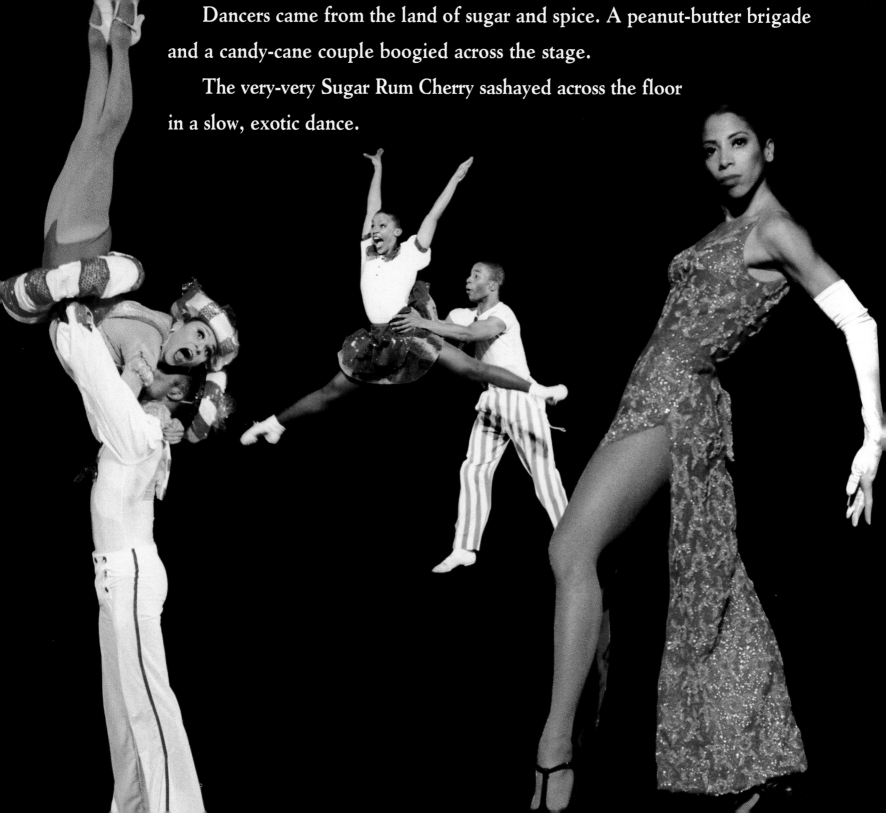

Dancers came from the land of sugar and spice. A peanut-butter brigade and a candy-cane couple boogied across the stage.

The very-very Sugar Rum Cherry sashayed across the floor in a slow, exotic dance.

The music swelled as delicate Chinoiserie took the stage with her man. A corps of beautiful flowers, along with one perfect Dewdrop, danced the Waltz of the Floreodores. Dancers from Arabia brought the crowd to their feet.

Clara wished she could stay at Club Sweets forever. But there was one act left.

Death, the grand finale, entered Club Sweets. Just as she had done when the magician called for a volunteer, Clara walked bravely onto the stage.

The hounds and the ghouls were nowhere to be found. Instead, Death was accompanied by ravishing dancers dressed in gold and pink, the colors of the sunset.

Club Sweets faded away as the dancers' pirouettes took Clara back in time, back to the events that had shaped her life.

First Death showed her the 1930s, when the Great Depression made everyone poor. Clara's home was filled with love. In that sense her family was very rich indeed.

She revisited the '40s. Gus proposed, then went off to fight the Second World War. Many courageous young men lost their lives, but Clara was fortunate—Gus returned safely.

The civil rights movement of the 1950s gave Gus and Clara hope for their family's future. No longer would anyone be forced to sit at the back of the bus, anywhere.

In the turbulent '60s, great changes sometimes brought great sorrow. Gus reacted violently when he heard about children killed in a Birmingham church. Clara worried that his rage would destroy their family.

A decade later, their son rebelled against his parents' belief in nonviolent change. But somehow Clara always bridged the gap of his anger with her love.

On to the '80s, the era of greed. Crack invaded Harlem. Homeless people begged in the streets.

Clara could not bear to relive the decline of her beloved neighborhood. "Enough! I've seen enough."

But Death was not through. The curtain opened to the 1990s and Gus's death.

"No-o-o . . ." Clara fainted into the arms of Death.

Morning light filtered through the French doors in the parlor on Sugar Hill. Clara lay on the floor where she had fainted the night before.

"Mother!" screamed Lakey. "Mother . . . Mother."

Lisa rushed in. "It's okay, Lakey, it's okay," she said. "Look. She's opening her eyes."

Lisa called to the men. Jamal and Thaddeus raced downstairs. "I'm okay, I'm fine," Clara insisted, as her children helped her to the sofa. "Let's not spoil Christmas for the children," she said, holding tight to her daughter.

With squeals of joy, the grandchildren stampeded downstairs, dived under the tree, and ripped open their gifts.

Lakey turned to her sister-in-law. "Thank you, Lisa. I don't know what I would have done if you hadn't been here." The women embraced each other. A flush of happiness filled Clara.

"Thanks for the truck!" Clara's youngest grandson ran to give his grandmother a kiss.

"You're very welcome." She softly cupped the boy's face in her hands. "I have something else for you, something special."

Clara reached for the nutcracker and gave it to her grandson. "I hope you'll cherish it for many Christmases to come."

"Oh, thank you, Grandma Clara!"

Once again, Clara sat alone on her sofa. But this time she no longer felt lonely. Her family was happy and together. It was Christmas. The nutcracker had been passed to a new generation. Her family's traditions would continue.

A mild breeze blew through the French doors. Once again Death entered the parlor. This time Clara was not afraid. She ran to its embrace. The face of Death and the huge black cloak fell away. In its place stood Gus.

Together, they climbed the stairway to eternity.
Clara took one last look at her family, then continued
her journey with her beloved prince.

"My grandmother raised me. This is my homage to her," says Donald Byrd.

In many ways his *Harlem Nutcracker* is an inversion of the traditional *Nutcracker* by E.T.A. Hoffmann. Donald Byrd's nutcracker is black, not white. Clara is old, not young. In place of the Land of Sugar, Grandmother Clara goes to the Harlem Renaissance – era nightclub, Club Sweets. The music is Ellington, not Tchaikovsky. The choreography is jazz dancing, not classical ballet.

But still, the values are similar. Both *Nutcracker*s are about family and tradition. And both *Nutcracker*s follow similar themes. In the original story the nutcracker fights the Mouse King and loses; Clara throws her shoe and kills the mouse. As Donald Byrd reinterprets it, the nutcracker fights Death and loses, and Clara shoves Death out the parlor door. "Somehow the nutcracker being in peril brings out that protective instinct in her," Donald explains. "Clara finds strength in defending someone who tried to protect her."

When the choreographer first heard Duke Ellington's interpretation of Tchaikovsky's *Nutcracker*, he was inspired by how "smart, witty, sophisticated, and urban it was." He decided to create a new *Nutcracker* around it. "I thought about what it would look like. Jazz is uniquely American. I knew that my ballet should be uniquely American, too.

"The traditional *Nutcracker* is pretty, but it isn't about us. I wanted to bring a sense of inclusion to African Americans. I wanted this *Nutcracker* to invite black people to the theater. That does not mean people of other ethnic groups cannot enjoy the ballet. If you can ask black people to relate to white people on the stage, I see no reason why white people should not relate to black people on the stage. It's really about inclusion.

"I knew that the grandmother had to be significant in the storytelling of *Harlem Nutcracker*. Grandmothers are very important in the African American community. They represent an ancestral link to Africa—a symbol of respect for one's elders and the honor for one's ancestors. Also, the grandparents carry forward the traditions of the church. The church in the black community is not just about religion. It represents community, morals, and ethics.

"There is a point in the show when all the children are gathered around Clara. It is so beautiful to see the love that these children have for this elderly woman. It's that bond between the seniors and the children, between the past and the present, between Africa and America."